WHEN A DRAGON COMES COURTING

A ROMANTIC FANTASY NOVELLA

TALES FROM KARNEESIA
BOOK ONE

CLAIRE TRELLA HILL

This book is a work of fiction. Names, characters, places, and incidents are the product of the author's imagination or are used fictitiously and are not to be construed as real. Any resemblance to actual events, locales, or persons, living or dead, is coincidental.

When a Dragon Comes Courting

Copyright © 2024 by Claire Trella Hill

Cover Art by JV Arts

Paperback ISBN: 979-8-9883463-2-6

All rights reserved.

For all the girls out there
who wouldn't mind a hot dragon man
I got you

CHAPTER
ONE

It was just barely spring when the soldiers arrived, dragging a man in chains into Roe's farmyard.

At the first sound of hooves, the chickens scattered, clucking their anxious protest at the disturbance of their routine. The gander hissed and flapped his wings, preparing to charge these intruders. Not many visitors found their way to her farm in this southern corner of Damaslar. It was too close to the sandy desert and the war being fought among the dunes.

Roe swatted the gander with her besom, and only her thick wool skirt protected her from his answering nip. He thought himself too much the protector of her household.

Then the riders came around the bend in the road, and she gripped the broom tighter, her knuckles turning white. Two squads of mounted army soldiers rode into her farmyard, road-weary and covered with trail dust. They had been riding hard and long, maybe all the way from the front, down in the sands of the Sarkan. But they weren't alone.

Their captain reined in his mount and gave a perfunctory look at his surroundings. "This will do." The disgruntled words rang through the air as he dismounted.

Roe's mouth dried. She had no trust for the army, and no sympathy—any stake she had had in their wars with the dragons had died with Sael.

A regiment had come through the year before and pressed all young and able-bodied men for the front, including her Sael. Roe got a notice barely a month later that the holy man had read to her. Sael had died for nothing—battle fodder for Damaslar's squabbles. It hadn't been a love match, but he had been good and steady, and she had cared for him. Now he was gone, leaving her and Aish alone.

What did these men want with her farm?

Aish yelled from inside the cottage and toddled out, holding onto their mutt Fang's thick gray fur. She tugged on her mother's skirts, shrieking her wordless demands.

Roe gathered up her two-year-old daughter in her arms and stared at the captain, who removed his helm and shook out sweaty hair the color of ripe wheat.

"Sword and *shield*, but this is the middle of nowhere." His pale blue gaze landed on her, and she inwardly quailed, hating the way his eyes licked over her.

"My name is Captain Andres Chevalier," he said. "My squads will be staying here to guard an important prisoner until wizards can arrive from the capital to take him the rest of the way."

Roe bit her lip and awkwardly dropped a curtsy while holding her toddler. "Sir, I cannot feed thirty men this early into spring," she whispered.

"They have rations," the captain said, waving a hand at his men. His eyes narrowed, searching behind her. "Where is your man?"

Her breath caught. Should she lie? Tell him that Sael was merely away? But who knew how long the soldiers would stay here, camped on her land? "In the desert," she said, voice cracking.

It was not technically a lie. Sael was in the desert, and there he would lie for eternity, buried in a mass grave or in the belly of a beast; she didn't know which.

"Ah," the captain said, one eyebrow quirking. "Well, be cheered, mistress. This prisoner may turn the tide of war for us. Your man'll be home to you before you know it." He waved his hand, and Roe took a good look at their captive for the first time.

The first things she noticed were the thick, heavy chains that wrapped around his arms and neck, carved with strange symbols she didn't understand. But after that, the prisoner was covered in blood and dirt… and naked.

She flinched involuntarily. "Who—"

"King's business." The captain strode forward and gripped her chin, forcing her to look up into his face. Fang snarled, but Roe made a hasty motion with her hand, signaling him to stay.

Captain Chevalier told her, "You will never speak of these events under pain of death, do you understand?"

Roe nodded rapidly. The grip on her chin tightened—and then a low growl rumbled through the farmyard, pulling her gaze like a lodestone to the prisoner.

The soldiers had forced him to his knees in the dirt, and his hands were chained behind his back, but the prisoner still managed to look powerful, even in a position of weakness. The incredibly broad and muscled chest contributed to that, probably. His tangled black hair and beard hung down to his bronze shoulders, and black eyes stared at her without a hint of white around them.

Roe gulped. She refused to let her gaze dip lower than his chest.

Captain Chevalier let go of her chin to ruffle Aish's hair. But her bossy two-year-old exclaimed "No!" as she was wont to do, since it was her favorite word, and slapped at the hand intruding on her person.

"Aish," Roe said hastily, stepping back and setting the girl down behind Fang, who positioned himself between his mistresses and danger. "Go and play, sweet. Go inside."

"No!" Aish said again, but went, herded by Fang.

"I expect supper at sunset," the captain said.

Roe looked up, startled. "But you said—"

"You won't cook for them," he said dismissively. "Just me."

And Roe felt afraid.

ROE COOKED supper and fed herself and Aish first, and then put her daughter in bed with her doll and Fang.

Then Captain Chevalier appeared in the doorway. He had washed, probably in the stream that ran along the fields, and his jaw showed signs of shaving.

Unease twisted in her stomach. "I would have brought your food to you—"

"I wanted to eat here, get away from the enlisted rabble for a while. Even though this cottage is incredibly rustic." The captain sat in the chair at the head of the table and stretched his legs out, watching her as she scurried to dish up another serving of stew.

She could feel his eye trailing over her form critically. She was little enough to look at, she knew—dark hair and dusky skin, as was the norm for their region, with a figure mostly hidden by her dress and surcoat. What little flesh she had at her disposal was quickly turned to muscle by farm chores and hard work. She let her hair, coming loose from its braids, hide her face.

"You don't know how it is at the front. All that damned sand. Roasting in your armor as you wait for a monster to attack." He dug into the stew, continuing to talk. "That's not to say we haven't bagged plenty of the beasts. There's many a skeleton bleaching white under that blasted sun." He smirked through a bite of stew.

Her stomach rolled in pity for the dragons.

He scratched his neck, a fleck of shaving soap still lingering under his ear. "But it's the same, day in and day out. I couldn't tell you what I felt when we saw the first real trees in months." He eyed her speculatively. "You don't talk much, do you?"

"Not really," Roe said, twisting her hands in her apron. "Only to the baby."

He glanced around the room. "Where is the brat?"

She stiffened. "In the back room. She's playing."

His eyelids lowered. "It must get lonely, so far out here. With only a child for company."

Her throat closed.

"It's lonely in the desert, too," he whispered, rising to his feet.

Her tongue stuck to the roof of her mouth as her stomach clenched in turmoil. Everything in her wanted to scream *no!* and reach for the iron fire poker, but he had thirty men right outside her door. Her baby was in the back room. He was stronger than her.

His hand slid over her cheek, down her neck, making her skin crawl.

Just—what if he hurts the baby—just don't feel—go somewhere else until he's done— Roe's fear filled her whole being as Captain Chevalier reached for her breast.

Then outside came a deep, bellowing roar.

"Captain!" A man yelled. "He's getting riled up—"

The captain cursed and stormed out of her cottage, leaving her shaking at the reprieve.

What sort of prisoner was this? She hovered in the doorway as six men held the end of the chains tight, barely managing to restrain the prisoner as he thrashed.

"Hold him, damn you!" Captain Chevalier screamed, pulling a sword from one of his men and striding forward. He set the blade against the prisoner's neck. "If you test me, beast, I'll cut off your balls and feed them to you for dinner! Don't think I won't!"

Roe took a step forward into the twilight as light from the torches lit the man's eyes, wide and black, void-pits of rage. Some of his wounds had reopened and wept rivulets of blood down his bronzed skin, which was already shiny with sweat.

"He looks fevered," she heard herself say.

Captain Chevalier swung around to look at her. "What?"

She struggled to speak with all eyes on her. "The wounds… they're fevering him. The mind will clear when the fever breaks."

"You have herb knowledge?"

She jerked a nod.

"Pour some noxious brew down his throat, then. Got anything to drug him senseless?"

She didn't, so she ignored the question. "To rid him of the fever fully, I'll have to clean those wounds," she whispered.

The soldiers—nearly fifteen, a whole *squad*—had finally wrestled the man to the ground.

What is *he*? Roe wondered again. *Deserter? Berserker? Sarkan'ande spy?* She knew the sand people fought with the terrifying beasts for the territory. And why not? Damaslar was the one who had invaded, wanting to control the desert and the trade routes to the far distant countries she had only vague knowledge of.

"You want to get up close and personal with the beast?" The captain spat, and she barely moved in time to avoid spittle on her boots. "Because that's what he is." He grabbed her arm and hauled her forward, discounting the growl that rattled forth deep in the prisoner's chest. "You'll never speak of this," the captain spoke into her ear. "Never. The knowledge is a secret to the crown. If you ever breathe a word of it, you and your daughter are dead instantly. Do you understand?"

Roe could barely breathe from the captain's horrible closeness and the oppressive waves of power the prisoner exuded, but she nodded, eyes pricking with tears.

"Here are the rules. Do not touch the chains for any reason. Don't get near his mouth; he bites. And do not let your foolish woman heart feel sorry for this," Captain Chevalier gestured. "Because this is the enemy. You may see flesh and blood, but inside?" He sneered. "That's a dragon in a man's guise."

THEY CHAINED the prisoner in the barn, thinking rightly that her skittish and frightened animals would alert them to any threatening move he made.

Of course soldiers wouldn't care if he managed to burn down my barn, Roe thought, gathering up bottles and unguents from her cottage with shaking hands.

He. It.

The dragon.

With a last hurried glance at her baby sleeping peacefully, Fang's ear clutched in her fist, Roe followed a soldier to her barn.

Two soldiers stood guard over the man—creature?—who sat in the straw, black-orbed eyes fixed on her approach. They had unwound the chains from him and brought his hands around to his front, tethering them to a stake they drove deep into the dirt floor.

She set her burdens down so she wouldn't drop them. After a nervous request for water, an irritated soldier brought her a bucketful, slopping some of it onto her skirts as he set it down. Then the soldiers went out and took positions at the barn door. So, they were not concerned about her safety, only the possibility of escape. A shiver ran down her spine at her vulnerability.

Roe wrung out a cloth and turned to the prisoner.

"I'm just going to—clean your wounds." Her voice cracked. She held out the cloth as evidence of her intentions.

The eyes didn't look away from her. They didn't even blink.

She swallowed and ran the cloth gently over one broad shoulder, crusted with dried blood from a sword cut. The prisoner seemed to exude heat; even though the cloth had been doused in cool water, it began to warm under her hand.

She did not want to think about the prisoner's warmth.

As more and more of him was washed and wounds cleaned, the more Roe suspected that warmth was his natural state. She revised her earlier opinion—he wasn't fevered from his wounds. He was....

Well, she didn't know what he was.

Eventually she had cleaned most of his chest and back. She handed him the cloth and moved the bucket closer, trying to keep the heat from her face. "You can, um...." she waved at the rest of him, her eyes on the salve she was opening. "I'll do this."

He dunked the cloth into the water, chains clinking. He wrung it out—and then grasped her wrist, pulling her forward with a hand that was missing all its nails.

Roe gasped, instinctively bracing herself on his uninjured shoulder. She stared down into eyes that frightened her with their intensity, and she flinched as he brought the cloth up to her face and rubbed.

"Something on my face?" she whispered faintly. His skin was so *hot.*

"The male." The words rumbled from him in a register so deep that it resonated in her bones. "He touched you."

She gulped. "What?"

"I smell him on you." Those piercing eyes blinked, clouded, and then cleared. The blackness receded from the corners, and a hint of white shone through. "His scent claim. But he has not mated you yet."

The captain's face flashed through her mind—his hand on her, the look in his eye. "No," she forced out, feeling sick. "Not if I can help it."

"Good." And the prisoner kept on rubbing her face and neck with the cloth. "Your other male is gone. His scent is very old, fading."

"Sael died," she said faintly, feeling adrift. "In the desert. They took him to fight their war. He didn't want to leave us."

The man made a sound in the back of his throat, a low thrum.

She took a breath and asked, "Are you really a dragon?" Although, with those eyes, how could she not believe it?

"Yes." He put the cloth down and cupped her face with two large, calloused hands, petting down her neck.

"What are you doing?"

His expression melded from intense to a more satisfied expression, one universal to males everywhere, regardless of what they were. "Claiming you."

CHAPTER
TWO

R oe lay in bed and stared up at the thatched roof of her cottage, touching her neck. Pressing her lips together, she breathed in the phantom scent of him, heat and musk mixed with some sort of spice that tickled her nose.

She still couldn't believe he had said that. And then an irritated soldier had broken the moment, declaring healing time to be over, and snatched her away by the arm. She didn't miss the prisoner's low parting growl.

Him. A dragon.

But that meant—that meant that the dragons of the desert weren't just mindless beasts. They took on human form. They spoke and reasoned. What would they do, those capital wizards, with a captive dragon?

Sael had never liked to see beasts chained. He fenced in their garden, barred the barn and chicken coop securely, but he never set traps unless he absolutely had to. *"We shouldn't blame wild things for being wild,"* he told her once. They were only acting according to their nature.

How much more then, an intelligent beast? Who took on a man's shape?

She rolled over in her bed and hugged her pillow to her chest, wishing Sael were here with her to tell her what to do. To stand against Captain Chevalier and his grasping hands. To reassure her with the steady comfort of his presence. But the army had taken him, and he was never coming back. That's all Damaslar ever did —take.

She drifted off to sleep only after her pillow had been liberally salted with tears.

IN THE VERY EARLY dawn light, she got Aish up and fed them both. Then she went about her chores quickly and quietly, Aish and Fang following behind her. The soldiers stationed at the barn doors—different ones from the night before—didn't pay her any attention.

She milked the cow and fed it and the horse. They were both still wary of the newcomer in the barn, but more settled. In the midst of mucking out the stalls, Roe heard Aish screech.

She was out of the stall in a second. "Aish—?"

Her daughter screeched again in wordless outrage that Fang would not let her closer to the stranger she so wanted to investigate. "No!" Aish exclaimed. "Mam!" She held up her hands.

Roe picked her up without protest. Aish kicked her heels as Roe settled her onto her hip.

The dragon man watched them both the whole time. "She is your kit," he said in his rough voice.

"Yes. She's called Aish. I'm Roe."

Hearing her name, Aish kicked harder. "Mam! Down!"

Used to the fickleness of the terrible twos, Roe lowered her. Fang again stepped between the stranger and Aish.

"Your beast—protects."

"Yes." Roe patted the dog's head. "It's all right, Fang."

In triumph, Aish darted around the dog and stumbled.

Quicker than sight, fast enough that Roe's hands barely had time to twitch, the dragon man steadied Aish, his chains clanking.

Roe held her breath as her heart beat a nervous time in her chest.

Aish beamed into his face, as though he had done something incredibly clever, and shrieked in delight, patting the hand that touched her with exquisite gentleness.

His eyes glowed. "Kits are rare. Precious."

Satisfied she had gotten to her quarry at last, Aish pulled away, off on another adventure. He let her go, steadying her steps as she toddled away, Fang following. Then his eyes met Roe's. She swallowed thickly.

The moment shattered when one of the guards banged open the barn door. "Best get out here. The captain's awake and wants his breakfast, quick like."

ROE HAULED A PROTESTING Aish out of the barn and back to the farmhouse, setting her down to play with some spoons and her doll while she dished up breakfast. Aish kept up a babbling commentary all the while, real words mixed in with babbling talk. As the porridge finished cooking, Roe sliced off a hunk of bread from her loaf—she'd need to bake more bread soon—and poured fresh milk into a cup. She put it all on a board that would do for a tray and met Captain Chevalier in the doorway as he prepared to enter.

"I thought it might be quieter for you outside," she murmured, as Aish shrieked to Fang, "No! Dolly sit! Fang!" and other incomprehensible babbles.

He cast a disgruntled look behind her and didn't bother to hide the curl of his lip. "Fine. Sit with me."

He had his men drag the low bench from her table out of the farmhouse and sat, balancing the board on his knee. Roe perched, sitting as far away from him as she dared on the bench as he shoveled the porridge into his mouth. "I can't wait to be back in the capital. Beast's *teeth* but I miss the food there," he mumbled, tearing a hunk out of the bread with his teeth, guzzling the milk.

Roe swallowed. "Why must you wait for these wizards?"

"They'll have better containment spells for the monster," he said around the food in his mouth. "And they'll help us find a way to ford the Lliore River. Running water destabilizes magic, you know."

She didn't, but what she knew concerning magic could've fit on the head of a pin.

"They're taking no chances with such a prize," he continued. "They'll want him absolutely secure, so the wizards have all the time they like to crack open his head and pull out his secrets."

"What secrets?" Roe whispered before she thought, but he kept talking.

"How to defeat the dragons down there in that poxy dune sea, and what sorcery lets them ape the guise of a man. How to spot them. What if all the sand scuts down there are dragons? But they can't be," he said, more to himself, "or they would've overrun us. But obviously they've got some treaty between them. Probably want all the gold for themselves."

"Gold?"

Captain Chevalier dunked the rest of his bread into his cup of milk and slurped at it. "Beyond the dunes, there are mines of gold and diamonds. Untold riches. Then past the desert are jungles and untapped lands, ripe for the taking. If we had more men, we could sweep down like a tidal wave."

Roe felt a chill wash over her. She gripped the fabric of her skirts tight to keep her hands from shaking.

More men. More men like Sael.

"We'll press the sand scuts into service, I don't doubt," the captain said, scraping the bottom of his bowl. "After we shoot all those overgrown lizards out of the sky." He stood up and dropped the board into her lap. "Decent enough breakfast. I expect my dinner at noon sharp."

When he walked back to his men to give them their orders for the day, Roe took the dishes inside and busied herself with scrubbing them to death as Aish tugged at her skirts, whining.

Then she dropped a carving knife into her apron pocket, picked up her daughter, and headed to the barn.

"Is it true?" she whispered, kneeling in front of him.

The dragon man lifted his head to meet her eyes with his. Something in the all-black depths glittered. "What?"

"That the army will… will torture you. Will sweep down through the desert with no check if the dragons are not there to stop them."

"Damaskmen." He made a derisive noise deep in his throat, then his face turned serious. "Single-minded. Violent. Driven by greed. Yes, it is possible. If no internal squabbles break out."

Internal squabbles like the virulent domestic wars and feuds that happened at least once a generation in different areas of Damaslar. Not to mention warlords that rose and fell with quick regularity. That was probably why the country had been forcefully set like an attack dog on the Sarkan. With no enemy to fight, Damaskmen turned on themselves.

"I don't want more men to die," Roe said, clasping her clammy hands together.

She didn't want *him* to die, either.

She looked over her shoulder. The soldiers on watch were just on the other side of the door. They all had weapons. They could kill her and Aish and not even blink.

"Tell me what I must do," she breathed, "to help you."

His eyes held hers for what seemed like an age, glittering like jet beads. She licked her lips, her mouth dry as bone while the rest of her sweated in fear.

"Brave," he whispered, touching her braid with the back of his fingers.

She shook her head. "Terrified."

A spark of humor crossed his face, the corner of his mouth twitching. "I must be free before the wizards come. Else they will take me back to a more magically protected stronghold, and I will never be free."

"What do you need?"

"Cut the runes to break the magic. Or pick the locks." He rattled his cuffs. "I cannot. They ripped away my talons."

Roe winced in sympathy for his ravaged hands. But...talons? "I have no skill with locks, but I have this." She drew the knife from her apron pocket.

"That will do. Cut deep, and all the way through the runes. The metal is silver, and softer than iron. There will be backlash, but I can absorb the greater portion. Dragons are good at that," he said, irony faint in his voice.

"They are?"

"Dragons hoard. Magic especially."

She gulped "And then that's it?"

He nodded. "Their wizards, they look for a way to protect the runes they cut from any interference such as this. But they have not found it yet." He smiled a small, harsh grin.

"Then what? What about the soldiers?"

From the black look on his face, she knew. Roe swallowed hard, a shiver running through her.

He assured her, "I will not hurt you or the kit. Is there a place where you can hide, where you are safe?"

"There's a root cellar in the house and another in the barn here."

"Get the kit and put her down there."

"Now?" she whispered.

He touched her face with one large hand. "Now. Before the male hurts you. He wants to. I can smell it on his scent. He will not touch you. Not while I live." His voice dropped to a growl. "Stay there until I come and find you."

"Aish," she called, voice shaking. "Come here to me." She

bundled her protesting child into the cellar, the dog close on her heels.

Climbing back up the ladder, Roe shifted her grip on the knife. "Just cut them?"

"Cut them," he said fiercely, holding the cuffs out.

With a deep breath, Roe dug the knife into the intricate symbols. She had to press hard to keep the blade from skittering away on the metal, but finally scored a cut through them.

On the second shackle, a rush of power exploded from the cuffs.

The blast knocked her backwards, forcing the air from her lungs. Before she could get her bearings, a terrible growl filled her ears. Metal snapped.

Big hands that grew bigger by the second scooped her up and stuffed her into the cellar, slamming the trapdoor.

"Mama!" Aish called. Roe fumbled for her daughter, clutching her as a deep bass roar penetrated the cellar.

Then the screams started.

Roe closed her ears against them as she hugged Aish close. *It was the right thing to do,* she thought, Fang whining with his tail between his legs, Aish wailing. *It was.*

But even the right thing can make you sick at heart.

A LONG TIME LATER, it was quiet. Aish had given up on crying and had fallen asleep in her lap. Roe stroked her hair softly. The trapdoor creaked, and she squinted against the light.

"They will trouble you no more."

Roe struggled to her feet, holding Aish, still out, against her shoulder. Fang kept close to her, growling as he smelled the blood and offal that coated the dragon man.

She took the steps slowly, staring at the picture of carnage he presented. He was so smeared with red she could barely see the bronze skin underneath. As wild and horrible as he looked, there was something different about his eyes, the tone of his voice.

Then she noticed the normal black pupils surrounded by white. The mad, fevered light was gone from his eyes, and his voice rang true and rich.

"What now?" she asked, sapped of strength.

"I will take the bodies away and cleanse your land with magic so no physical or magical trace will be left. No one will connect you with soldiers that disappeared or a dragon that escaped." He reached out one finger, as if to touch the roundness of Aish's cheek in sleep, but he stopped before the grime on his hands coated her. "Thank you for freeing me from my chains," he said. "They would have driven me mad. They nearly did. I owe you a life debt."

The words swam through her head with little meaning. She swayed on her feet.

"Go and sleep," he urged, his eyes consuming her. "I will take care of everything."

She could've argued, but she didn't. Roe went to the farmhouse, looking nowhere except where she'd place her next step. She fell into bed, Aish with her, and slept the deep sleep of exhaustion.

When she woke, it was to Aish's insistent pokes on her face and the chant, "Mam! Dindin! Mam! Dindin!"

Roe passed a hand over her face, and then shot up. Bolting out of her door, Roe stared at the farmyard—green, calm, the chickens and geese clucking peacefully. No signs of fighting or carnage. Completely empty.

The dragon had gone.

CHAPTER

THREE

Aish was deeply embroiled in a fierce battle with the goat when Fang whined in the back of his throat. But she couldn't spare a thought for him now. The nanny goat had decided that she absolutely, positively, without question, did not want to be milked.

Foolish, Aish thought, as if the milk would magically disappear from the teats by itself. All she'd gain by contrariness would be pain and a tight udder.

But the nanny was missing her kid, which Mam had sold earlier in the week. Aish hoped it had gone to a farmer that would raise it and breed it, but she was afraid that wasn't so. Because of the drought, the whole area was short of food. The last of their demesne's meager resources had gone to celebrations earlier in the year, to celebrate the "victorious Damaslar army."

Mam had huffed and mumbled bad words under her breath at that, since no one had really been victorious in the Dragon Wars. Damaslar had fought and battled over the desert for eight years, and all that had come out of it was that they now had a tenuous claim to the city-state of Darikar, and that the Sarkan'ande, the desert people, hated the Damaslar plainsmen more than ever before.

The last couple of years there wasn't even much fighting, just skirmishes here and there and an increasingly vocal army fed up with being dug into the desert sands, waiting for threats they could not anticipate. When some conflict boiled over in the north that required arms and resources, the king pushed the peace treaty through.

"Serves them right," Mam had muttered on the day they had learned the war was at an end. Aish's pa had died in the war, which was why Mam hated the army so.

Aish understood. Sometimes late at night, she would get a tight feeling in her chest when she thought about having no memory of her pa. Even so, she had been loath to miss what little celebrations their village had put together, but Mam had forbidden her to go.

And now there was no time to go gallivanting off to the village. Aish knew things weren't good on their farm, or with any of their neighbors'. It was too dry. The corn was withering and baking in the fields before it was time to harvest. Even their land, which had produced wildly and abundantly for as long as she could remember, was turning brown and brittle with no rain.

If they couldn't get a good crop in, the magistrate of the district might call in their debts and take their farm. Worse, they could be indentured, like the Coopers had been when they had run out of items to pawn or trade, and sent far, far away to work for strangers until their debt was paid.

Mam had told her the stories of growing up with too many brothers and sisters to feed, barely eking out enough food to live, terrified that what little they had would be taken. Aish shuddered just thinking of it, even in the heat.

Aish didn't know any of Mam's family. When Mam married Aish's pa, she was much better off because Pa's brother and sister had died of influenza when he was a child. He was the sole inheritor of the farm. But Mam's worthless pa—that's what she called him whenever she spoke of him because he had had it bad for the drink—and the brothers and sisters left who were just like him always came around making trouble, expecting help.

After the first few times, Aish's pa had told them he could hire them on and pay them a wage for their work, but he wasn't going to watch them piss away his coin for nothing. They hadn't liked that. Most of them drifted away, and the others were drafted into the war and died in the sand.

Most of the time Aish didn't mind, since Mam clearly didn't, but sometimes she thought a little wistfully of cousins her own age, and games and laughter. But given the choice, she'd rather have a pa.

But she didn't have a choice, so she got neither.

The nanny kicked the milk pail again, so Aish had to get her turned around, right the bucket, try to milk her all over again—nothing was ever easy. Aish hated feeling helpless, like nothing she did helped. But she was nine—nearly ten, she corrected herself—and she could milk the goat, so come hell or high water, she'd milk the thrice-cursed goat.

Just as she got her situated, the nanny bleated and her head shot up, going from stubborn insistence to blind panic in a second. Ripping the lead out of Aish's hold, the nanny bolted for the safety of the barn and her stall, knocking Aish on her backside in the dirt.

Wincing at the pain in her palms, Aish got to her feet, shaking out her skirt and brushing the dirt from her surcoat, ready to yell a word Mam did not realize Aish knew.

Then she froze.

Coming towards her on the road strode a man, tall and broad, with dark hair that shone in the sun and bronze skin, a darker cast than most of the folk from their region. He wore clothes of good quality, though dusty from traveling, and carried a pack on his back.

Fang, strangely enough, wagged his tail, though he kept it tucked close to his backside, and padded to meet the man.

The stranger stroked the dog's muzzle, the gray shot with white hairs, and rumbled something that made Fang's tail wag faster. Then he looked up and met Aish's eyes.

She gulped. "Hello. Are you looking for work?"

The man said nothing.

"It's just that if you are, you might have more luck further north," Aish continued bravely. "I don't think we could pay you, though we might be able to feed you." If she could get the blasted goat milked. What had startled the nanny that badly? "You'll have to ask my mam."

The man straightened. White teeth glinted in his close-cut beard as he flashed her a startling smile. "You have grown up, little one," he said in a warm, low voice.

For a moment, Aish's world tilted, and she thought that the pa from Mam's stories had come alive again. *But that couldn't be true,* she told herself sternly as she tried to remember how to breathe.

But how did the man know her? Who was he?

"Aish? Haven't you got the milk yet?" Mam said, coming out of the farmhouse, broom in hand. "I—"

Her words died at the sight of the man.

"It's you?" Mam said, stunned, like she did not really believe it.

"Yes," the man said firmly. "The war has ended. I have come to repay my debt."

Aish looked between them, bewilderment building in her chest. "Mam?"

Her mother stepped forward and took her hand. "Aish, this is —" She stopped, bemused, and exchanged a look with the stranger.

"I am called Galad," the man said, "and when you were very small, your mam did me a very great favor, and now I have come back to repay her."

"Oh," Aish said. "But I don't remember you."

"You would not," the man said, voice dry. "You were this tall." He held his palm up at the height of his knee. "A small kit. And this one was young." He patted Fang again, who wagged his tail and whined happily, nearly crawling on his belly. Aish blinked at the sight.

"Aish, will you go and finish with the nanny, and then set another place for breakfast?" Mam said. "I want to talk with Galad."

Aish drifted back to the barn, casting glances over her shoulder every few steps at the stranger. She didn't want to lose sight of him for a moment.

ROE STEPPED FORWARDS, taking in the strength of the man, his power. For half a second, she thought he might have stepped directly from her memories, he looked so unchanged.

But in her memories, the dragon man didn't wear clothes.

"You came back." She hugged her shawl around her body as Fang pranced around them both.

"I did," he rumbled, his gaze settling over her like a physical touch. His attention made her shiver.

She swallowed. "It has been a long time."

"I could not leave my people until the war was won and peace secured," he said. "And I forget how quickly time runs for humans. I am sorry for it."

"I'm surprised you remembered."

His eyes, she noted, were not the black, feverish pits from her memory. They looked perfectly normal, in fact. If normal dark eyes had specks of gold that glowed faintly, that is.

"How could I forget?"

She nodded jerkily. "So."

Very softly, he said, "There is still no male."

Her lips parted, but no words came. Her cheeks flushed, and she looked away. She couldn't deny the truth. There had never been another after Sael. She had had a few offers over the years, but she had never needed a man to help her with the farm longer than a few weeks at harvest time, and no offer had tempted her.

Not with the memory of a naked dragon man in her barn.

"So," he said, and lifted a hand. The pad of his thumb ran over her cheekbone, rough and strong. The heat pulsed from his skin— that had not changed. But fingers that had had nails ripped from their beds now sported sharp, wicked points.

But he was careful. The claw never touched her, skimming over her skin with the lightest grace imaginable.

She reached up and took his hand, turning it over between her palms. "They grew back?"

"Yes. I am fully restored."

She hurriedly let go, a shiver passing through her.

"So, you have come here, to, to—"

"To pay back the debt I owe you."

Her stomach dropped, but she refused to interrogate why. "Yes. Of course. But I really don't see…." She cast around at her farm, the animals left, the far fields wilting under the glaze of sun.

"I am here to help you in any way I can," the dragon man said. "Tell me, Roe. Tell me what you need."

FOUR

"Is he staying, Mam?" Aish whispered when her mother returned with the strange man called Galad. Her mother nodded, busy dishing up the breakfast things.

"But where will he sleep?"

"In the barn."

"Have we got anything to pay him?"

"He doesn't want paying. He's here to repay us."

"What did you do, that he's come back so many years later?" Aish asked curiously.

But Mam told her to sit down and eat and not ask so many questions.

Over breakfast, Aish stared at the large stranger that sat across from her at the table. He looked like he could eat a whole chicken on his own, maybe even *two* chickens, but he ate his small bowl of porridge without complaint, silently refusing the bread Mam offered him.

"It's good goat's milk," Aish finally offered.

"And you vanquished the goat?" he said, his lips curling up in a smile.

"Yes. She was just fine in the barn." Aish frowned. "Why was she so scared of you?"

"Strangers frighten animals sometimes," he said vaguely.

She didn't think that was the case, because sometimes on market day they brought the nanny into the village and milked her for a penny a cup, and she had never been frightened then. Grouchy and truculent, yes, but not frightened.

He swallowed his cup of goat's milk in one long gulp and stood, making the room feel very small. "I will have a look at the fields," he told Mam, who just nodded. Then he was out the door.

"Go look at the fields?" Aish repeated incredulously. "What does he mean? He's no farmer, Mam; he looks more like—"

"You've got a long list of chores to get through, miss, so best be about it," her mother said, handing her the broom. "And I want to hear no more chattering about Galad."

Aish groaned but began to sweep.

THEY SAW NO MORE of the stranger that day, though Aish kept sticking her head out the door so often to look for him that Mam said she'd get a crick in it.

He reappeared around the evening meal in time to help Aish haul water and stoke the kitchen fire, and after they ate, he brought in the plow horse's tack from the barn and mended it as Aish hemmed an apron, her summer sewing project, and Mam wove by firelight. When it was full dark, he slipped out the door to the barn with only a few murmured words.

As the door whispered closed, Mam called, "Wait!" and jumped up. She bundled up several blankets and the pillow Aish had made last year into a pile and set them in his arms. "To make your stay more—comfortable," Mam stammered.

His eyes gleamed as he took the blankets from her. "Thank you, Roe," he murmured in a voice like smoke. Then he was gone.

IN THE MORNING when she woke, Aish found water waiting for her without having to walk to the stream, a fresh fire burning merrily on the hearth, and the stranger in the process of mucking out the few stalls the animals used.

Aish collected the eggs from the chickens and ferried them safely to the house before rolling up her sleeves and preparing to battle the nanny. But she found Galad waiting for her, holding the nanny's lead rope as the goat alternately shivered and glared.

"I can do it, you know," Aish grumbled, swiping hair from her eyes. She had not put her hair in plaits yet. Mam would fuss at her for it, especially since she had more time this morning from his help.

"I know it," he rumbled. "The goat does not."

Aish frowned but brought the milking stool and bucket. The nanny stood still for her to get a pail full of milk, but as soon as the pail was sloshing at the rim, she bolted for the safety of her barn stall. Galad let her go and wound up the lead rope in his hand.

Aish goggled. "How did you untie it so fast?"

"I have quick hands," he said, and smiled.

AFTER BREAKFAST, Galad disappeared again, to Aish's great disappointment. At midmorning, after doing her chores—well, most of them—Aish finally escaped from the house and made her way to the fields, full of brown corn stalks that whispered in the dry wind. Sometimes she wondered if it was brittle enough a strong enough wind would take the crop and turn it into dust and chaff. This was Damaslar, the land fertile enough that you could plant a gold coin and a money tree would come up, or so the oldsters in the village said. But even fertile land couldn't compete against this long a drought.

Through the waving, rustling strands, she found Galad's head and shoulders as he walked through the fields, sometimes bending over, then straightening again and moving on. When he reached the end of a row, she met him, asking, "What are you doing?"

"Strengthening the crops." He touched the bottom stalk and slowly drew his hands up the stalk to where the ears were trying to mature.

"By touching them?" Aish made a face. "You'd be better off trying to water them. If we don't get rain, Mam thinks we might lose the crop."

He shook his head. "Your stream is very low, and the ground is too dry. It would disappear in an instant and do little good."

"I know; that's why we haven't tried it. We can't water the whole field anyway."

She watched his bronze hands stroke the drying leaves. "Many things are strengthened by touch," he said. "Have you not been encouraged by a hand on your shoulder at a time of need?"

Or a hug, Aish thought, like when she dropped a dish and Mam had held her to assure her it was all right. Right after commanding her not to move while she swept lest Aish step on the shards.

Aish nodded to show she understood, and Galad made a sound of assent.

His manner of speaking was odd. His words had different stresses, different from the folk in their village and from the merchant caravans that sometimes passed through. She gathered a breath and asked, "Where are you from?"

He kept his eyes on the corn as he replied. "The south. Desert country."

"My pa died there." Aish mulled this over. "Were you in the war?"

"Yes."

"Did you ever see a dragon?"

He smiled as he straightened to his full height. "Many times."

"How big was it?"

"Bigger than your cottage."

She stared at him in awe and maybe a little bit of fear.

He cocked his head. "Do you want to hear about dragons?"

She twisted her hands in her apron, casting a guilty look over her shoulder. "Maybe later," she said reluctantly, "I have to finish chores."

He set his hand on her head. "You are a good kit."

She could feel the heat from his hand even through her hair. It was heavy and comforting. She had the funny thought that maybe he had mistaken her for a wilting cornstalk.

When he moved his hand from her hair, she stared at the broad, scarred hands. His nails were dark, and wickedly sharp.

"Why don't I remember you?" she said again, feeling like she was in a dream.

"You were very small. Barely speaking. Your hound remembers."

Aish turned to see Fang approaching, nearly on his belly, tail wagging madly.

Galad patted his leg, and Fang bounded forward, whining happily as Galad scratched his head and ran his hands over the dog's back.

"He hasn't done that in a long time," she said in surprise. "He's got hip problems."

Galad's lips curved in a quiet smile.

Aish crossed her arms over her chest. "You said you were in the war. What were you doing here, then? How did you meet us?"

"Your mother will be the one to tell you."

"She told me to stop asking questions."

Galad let out a sigh, strong enough that it reached Aish. It felt like the heat from the oven fire. "Your mother helped me at a time of desperate need, at great danger to herself. Let her tell you when she is ready."

Aish felt the blood drain out of her head. Her fingers felt icy, even under the hot sun. "Does this have something to do with the body buried in the south field?" she whispered.

He looked up sharply. "What?"

"Last year, at plowing time. We found… bones." From a shoulder and a leg. She still remembered the white look on Mam's face when the plow unearthed the yellow bones. "Mam said that the land just moves things around, like rocks that show up every year in fields we've plowed clean the year before, and it was probably from some battle hundreds of years ago… but she didn't finish plowing that day."

"Ah," he said in a low voice. "The quirk of the Damaslar soil. I had forgotten. Where are the bones now?"

"Mam reburied them at the edge of the field."

He nodded. "Don't worry, little one. I will put the bones to rest. They will not trouble you again."

Mam's voice drifted over the fields, sounding exasperated. "Aish! Aish, I want you to come bake the bread. Where are you?"

"I'd better go," Aish said reluctantly.

Galad gave her a smile and a little push in the direction of the house. "Bake the bread. I look forward to trying it tonight."

FIVE

The house had echoed with Aish's refrains of "how?" and "Why?" and "but I want to *know*" all day, and now Roe had a headache. She pressed her fingers to her forehead, trying to relieve the tension in her head and in her neck and shoulders.

Fielding Aish's questions had grown exponentially more difficult today. Galad had said something to her, she knew it. Roe's excuses and vague answers had worn increasingly thin. Aish eventually had demanded, "Why won't you *tell* me what happened?"

To which Roe had no answer.

What had happened to her straight face? Roe had perfected the simple, befuddled expression years ago when wizards had arrived, searching for squads that had disappeared, and it had worked. A few questions put to a tired, ignorant woman and they had no doubt that soldiers had been nowhere near her farm. What would she know about troop movements? She rarely saw strangers in her village. Rarely saw anyone since the start of the war. She had asked nothing about their quest, thinking that any sign of curiosity might be suspect. And off they had gone down the road again, and never came back.

Never mind that she had collapsed into a shaking heap once the last trace of their dust had disappeared, and she hadn't managed to do anything else that day except hold Aish tight to her, even as the two-year-old had protested.

The real answer to Aish's question was that Roe had never spoken of it, had buried the incident in her memory. It only returned to her in fragmented dreams late at night, of screams and roars and blood… and large hands that stroked down her neck and shoulders, sending hot tingles through her as a voice whispered, *"claiming you."*

Roe ground her knuckle into her eye socket as Aish started up again. "Mam, why can't you just tell me what happened!"

A rumble cut through her whine. "I did not tell you to badger your mother to death, kit. Go and draw the water."

"But—"

His voice lowered. "Now."

A pause, and then Aish's footsteps plodded sullenly away. Roe breathed a sigh of relief.

Hands settled on Roe's shoulders, and she jumped.

"Peace," Galad said. "I am sorry. I did not realize how inquisitive and insistent kits are. Or perhaps it is just yours that is so strong-willed." His hands dug into her muscles, massaging away the aches and tension.

Roe let out a small moan as he worked his way from her shoulders to the back of her neck, and then down her spine to the small of her back, pressing into the knots and working them away. His hands were nearly magic, they were so warm and strong. Before she knew it, she was limp against him, and he was holding her up.

"Feel better?" he whispered.

Roe's eyes shot open, and she straightened hurriedly. "Y-yes."

He smiled, his eyes glowing.

Aish scraped in the door, setting down sloshing buckets full of water and unhooking the yoke from her shoulders. "Here," she said sullenly.

"Will you apologize to your mother?"

Aish glared. "You're not my pa!"

"You think only your father can tell you to respect your mother?"

Glancing between Galad and Roe, Aish's expression grew uncertain, then crumpled. "I'm sorry, Mam."

Roe folded her daughter into her arms rocked her as she cried a little. "I'm sorry, too," Roe whispered. "I didn't know how to talk about it, and I haven't wanted to because it is dangerous. But after supper, I'll tell you what I can. How is that?"

Aish sniffed into her surcoat and nodded. Then, to Roe's surprise, Aish pulled away from her and threw her arms around Galad. "I'm sorry too."

"There, now," Galad murmured. "No more sorrow."

AFTER SUPPER, Aish sat on her hands and said, "I promise I won't interrupt you, Mam. You can tell it how you want."

"No questions?" Roe teased with a ghost of a smile. "The world might be ending."

Aish giggled, wriggling in anticipation.

Roe sobered, trying to think of where to start. "It was the spring of your second year," she finally said. "The war had been on for a little more than a year." Aish nodded.

"Soldiers came to our farm with a prisoner in chains," Roe said slowly. "It was Galad."

Aish's eyes grew wide as she stared at Galad across the table. "So, you were on the Sarkan side?"

He nodded. He met Roe's eyes. He'd let her tell it how she liked.

"I was angry at the army—at the country. Your pa died only a month after they took him. And having two squads of soldiers show up at our farm didn't help. They were waiting here for wizards to arrive and take Galad away and interrogate him.

Torture him. And the captain in charge was horrible. He scared me." She shot a look at Galad. "You acted out to distract him."

"Yes." The word was so deep she could barely discern the syllables.

"I helped Galad escape," she told Aish. "What I did was treason. That's why I didn't want to tell you. You were safer not knowing."

Aish mulled this over with wide eyes. "That's why you couldn't come back until the war was over?" she asked Galad. He nodded. "And the... bones?" she whispered, her gaze flickering between them.

"Bones?" Roe said.

Galad said firmly, "Your mother had nothing to do with the bones." He set a hand on Aish's hair, which Roe noted was straggling out of her halfhearted plaits. "I dealt with them. You do not need to think of them again."

"What happens to people who commit treason?" Aish asked.

Roe bit her lip.

"Nothing," Galad said firmly.

Roe stopped breathing.

"Because I will not let anything happen to you or your mother," he continued.

"You promise?"

"My word on this, little one."

ROE WATCHED the fire pop and snap in the hearth after Aish had climbed into the loft to sleep. "Was I right to keep your secret from her?"

Out of the corner of her eye, she saw Galad shrug. "I do not consider it a secret."

She blinked, started. "You don't?"

He raised an eyebrow at her. "No. I am always a dragon, no matter what form I wear." While she processed that, he continued,

"I have walked the boundary lines of your land. I believe I can rejuvenate your fields."

Roe sat up straight. "How?"

"With magic."

"You can do magic?"

He turned and gave her a patently obvious look.

"Oh. Right." She flushed and swallowed, glancing back towards the dancing flames. "Why did you really come here, Galad? It wasn't to do farm chores."

"I had placed a charm on the land before, when I hid the bodies. I buried them deep, but Aish told me you found one. I am sorry for it."

"That's what you meant by bones?" An involuntary shiver rocked her as she recalled the yellowed bones, their appearance in a field she had sworn plowed clean for the past seven years. The ragged end of the leg bone, hewn off by teeth or claw. She shook her head. "No, that's... I made a choice. I knew what the consequences would be, and I don't regret it. I just... thought you ate them. What sort of charm was it?"

He sat up very straight, his eyebrows shooting up. "Dragons do *not* eat humans," he said in a very flat voice.

She blinked, taken aback. "There was a lot of blood. I remember." The whole farmyard had been coated in it, as had he.

After a moment, he unbent a tad. "Perhaps in battle, during the tearing and rending of enemies," he conceded finally, "but dragons do not consider humans a food source. And I was not myself at that time. The wizard enchantments placed on the chains had driven me half-mad. If you had not released me when you did, I think I would have gone truly insane. I do not know what kind of harm I might have caused, or what the wizards would have forced me to do."

She nodded, more than a little relieved. She had always believed it was so, that he was being deeply harmed by the chains, and now here she had proof. "And the charm?"

"The charm was for fruitful harvests. Bountiful crops." He

stroked his beard meditatively, the nails clicking together. "It was fortuitous that peace was achieved this year. I could feel the charm fading."

She leaned back in her chair, befuddled. "What on earth made you decide, 'oh, before my journey home, I should charm a stranger's land'?"

He lifted his gaze to meet hers. His look was warm, and very pointed. "I wanted to provide for you. Wanted to make sure you were cared for."

She gulped. "And so you came back to renew the charm."

He shook his head.

"Then… what?

"I came back for you."

Her heart began to beat rapidly, thrumming in her chest. She could not look away from his intense, burning eyes.

"Dragons," he said, "Are different."

"I've noticed," she croaked, trying to wet dry lips.

"Around mating," he said gently.

She nearly squeaked. "H-how so?"

"A male will put his claim on a female, and if she does not dispute it, he will begin providing for her, proving his worth. He will accomplish whatever task she sets before him, perform acts of service to be taken into consideration for life mate status. He will even duel his competitors if she asks. There is fierce competition between males for mating," he added, seeing Roe's shocked look. "I know humans choose their mates differently. You would not have understood what I did, and upon my return, I was braced to find you had taken another—"

"What?" she exclaimed. "You mean when you—" She blushed and fluttered her hands over her shoulders.

He nodded in confirmation, eyes glowing like coals. "Even half out of my mind, I wanted you. In the years since, you have filled my dreams, Roe. If you let me, I would bring your crops back to life, fill your streams with clear water, give you only good things for all of our days."

Shockingly, Roe felt her eyes suddenly fill with tears. No one had ever said anything so... so romantic to her. "Why *me*?" she forced out in a thin and wavering voice. "Are there no dragon women in your land? I'm human, and a very poor specimen," she said, waving to herself. "There are far better and more beautiful women—"

Galad came to his feet and pulled her upright from her chair. "*No*," he declared. "I want no other. I saw you, Roe. I saw you, alone, in danger. Yet you extended compassion to me. You washed my wounds when you did not have to. You were brave and good. In my maddened state I claimed you to protect you from an evil male, but I realized I claimed you for myself far more.

"I want this. I want you. After years of war, I crave the simplicity of caring for you, and Aish, and the animals, and the land. I came here knowing you might turn me away utterly, or have forgotten me, but did so just the same. Even now, I place no burdens on you. If you tell me to go, I will. If you tell me to wait, I will wait with the patience of the stream and the river for a bend to approach."

She hiccupped. "Water has the t-tendency to wear things down."

He smiled, a slow, toe-curling expression. "I still have a decent understanding of strategy. I can be tactically patient."

"You really would give up your home, your people, for this?" She gestured helplessly to her farmstead, which had always felt small and rude, for all its practical sturdiness.

He cupped her face in his hands. "If you are here, it is the whole world to me."

She lost the battle against the tears she had been fighting, and two slipped down her cheeks. With his thumbs, he smoothed the streaks of water away, mindful of his claws. Then, with aching gentleness, he pressed his lips to hers.

She clung to his arms as she lost herself in the sensation of heat, with occasional scrapes of beard against her skin that sent tingles through her. When Roe came back to herself, she found herself clutched against Galad's hard form with his hand stroking her back as he pressed kisses into her hair.

"Does this mean I'm considering you?" she said a bit muzzily.

His hand on her back paused. "If you say it does," he murmured.

"Oh, good," she whispered, and lifted her face to kiss him again. A moment later, she pulled back and asked, "But what about the differences?"

Galad blinked. "What differences?"

"The dragon differences. Around mating. I didn't think that you looked too different from a human male. Not that I was looking," she assured him hurriedly.

Galad stared at her and abruptly burst into laughter.

"What?" she demanded, and when he clarified between gasps of mirth: "Well, you can understand why I thought—Galad, stop laughing; it's not *that* funny!!"

CHAPTER

SIX

In the gray pre-dawn light, Aish poked her head over the lip of the loft and blinked blearily. She didn't want to get up, and sleepily hoped Galad would come and take care of things for her again, so she wouldn't have to.

The door opened, admitting the murky half-light as well as a large form. Aish yawned slowly as the figure knelt by the hearth and piled logs in the fireplace.

Needs kindling first, Aish thought sleepily.

But the figure did not reach for the kindling. He leaned forward and breathed on the wood in the hearth, and a ribbon of fire flared out from his mouth. The wood caught and began to burn.

Aish froze, her heart pounding as the figure coaxed the flame higher before picking up the water buckets and yoke and exiting the house. Her mind whirled, trying to process what she had seen. It didn't seem possible. Maybe Galad was a wizard who could do magic. But everyone knew that human wizards used magical runes to write down what they wanted their magic to accomplish, and Galad hadn't written anything. He had just… breathed.

She puzzled over it as she dressed and did her plaits and went downstairs and lit the lamps.

During breakfast, Mam remarked on her quietness, and brushed a hand over Aish's forehead. "Did you not sleep, sweet?"

Aish shook her head.

Galad put his hand on her head. Aish looked up at him and felt a cool, refreshing sensation fill her. "She is fine," Galad said. "Just quiet this morning, hmm?"

"I guess," she murmured into her cup.

She wasn't stupid. She knew there were things Mam and Galad had left out of their story. For one thing, two squads was a lot of soldiers, wasn't it? Probably at least ten? How would Galad have —Aish gulped—gotten *rid* of all of them, with no help from Mam? Even with magic, that seemed like a large feat.

And Mam had never said, but Galad must have magic. Why would some old capital wizards be interested in him if he was just a regular Sarkan'ande soldier? So, he used magic, but he wasn't a wizard. So, he was... he was....

Aish gulped again.

<hr>

Aish couldn't escape from her chores until the afternoon, but once she did, she didn't have to hunt for Galad—he was in the barn, doing repairs on some of the stall walls and doors. She leaned over the top of the stall and watched him hammer nails into the wood, patching the holes.

"You said a dragon was as big as our house," she said abruptly.

He looked up from where he was crouched. He did not seem surprised by her sudden appearance. "Yes."

"What else do they look like?"

He raised an eyebrow.

"I've just heard what people say," she said hurriedly. "Big and winged and all the teeth... but how can something that big fly?"

"Magic."

She blinked.

"You think beings that breathe living flame aren't full of magic?" The corner of his mouth turned up.

"And they don't singe their feathers?"

Galad threw back his head and laughed, an expression of delight crossing his face. "No, dragons have wings more like a bat," he explained, showing her with the flesh between his thumb and first finger what he meant. "The membrane is thin but very tough, able to withstand much but delicate enough to catch the breeze and hold them aloft. The rest of the dragon is protected with skin like extremely tough leather that protects against flame and fang and claw."

"No scales?"

He shook his head. "In some places the skin texture is so hard and horny that it may resemble scale patterns, but not truly scales. What if they had to shed like a snake? It would be very undignified." He smiled.

"What if another dragon bites their wing? Is it not protected?"

He stiffened. "No dragon would," he said in a flat voice. "It is the height of dishonor. No dragon wants to be so shamed."

Aish stared at him as he pounded nails with a vengeance into the wood.

Animals didn't have honor. They only had instinct, and animals in a fight went for any advantage. Galad spoke as if dragons were people. He was *angry* about the idea that a dragon might do something so... taboo.

He was hot all the time.

His fingernails were too sharp.

He breathed *fire* into the hearth this morning.

Galad paused in his hammering and swiped a sleeve over his forehead. He looked up. And he saw the knowledge in her face.

He—stopped moving, the way wild things do when they realize you're watching them, poised to bolt if you make the slightest twitch. So Aish held her breath, and nearly went cross-eyed trying not to blink, and finally, Galad very slowly set the hammer down.

Oh, Aish realized. *He's worried he's frightened* me.

She licked her lips and very slowly said, "Well, if dragons are as big as a house, where does the rest of you get to like this?"

Galad's eyes lost some of their starkness, the warm flooding back in. One eye slowly winked at her. "Magic."

AFTER THAT, Aish thought that Galad might've regretted admitting to being a dragon, because she refused to shut up about it. She trailed him for the next hour as he did his repairs, insisting, "but I want to *seeeeee!*"

A great fantastical thing the likes of which she'd heard of only in stories, and he was here! In the flesh! Well, most of it. How could she let that rest until she saw it?

She wheedled and begged until he finally gave in. Galad put down his tools and walked into the fields they had let lie fallow this year. "You are persistent for a tiny kit," Galad mock-growled. "Like grains of sand scratching against my hide, scouring away my skin."

"So, you're going to change?"

"Yes, you single-minded pestilence."

Aish cheered.

When they reached the far field, out of sight of the house, Galad began to disrobe unselfconsciously, pulling his tunic and shirt over his head and yanking off his boots. Aish squeaked and spun around.

"Peace," Galad chuckled. "I will not take off my smalls."

Aish turned back around slowly, peeking between her fingers. Galad stared up at the sky, the sun shining into his face, making his eyes glow. Aish squinted against the brightness. The sun was shining right into her eyes—no, not the sun, but... was Galad glowing? Yes, he was, so brightly she almost couldn't look at him.

Aish covered her eyes against a great flash. A whiff of cinnamon, a spice she had smelled only rarely when traders came through, entered her nose. Something rustled.

Hesitantly, Aish cracked her eyes open. Then they flew wide.

Molten gold eyes stared at her calmly from a creature that—*yes*—was as large as their house, or even bigger if you took into account the bronze-and-green wings folded carefully down its back. "Galad?" Aish squeaked.

The lips curled in a dragon facsimile of a smile, giving her a good view of sharp white teeth. "Yessss?"

Her jaw dropped. "You can *talk*?"

One huge shoulder shrugged. "In thissss form—diffffficult. But not imposssssssible."

Aish did a slow circuit around Galad, staring at the muscles that rippled under the bronze hide, the wicked-looking talons that emerged from his feet, and the barbed end of the tail she was careful to stay away from. She hesitantly reached out a hand and touched his shoulder. He was warm, like a hearthstone. She had a small, hysterical thought that if she cracked an egg over him, he might be hot enough to cook it.

Galad's head and neck snaked around at her giggle, examining her with faint amusement through one huge golden eye. "Sssssssatisfied?"

"Yes." Impulsively, Aish threw her arms around as much of Galad's neck as she could reach. She felt a hot, bright burst, and then the thick, corded muscle under her became fluid, shifting and changing in an instant. Instead of hot dragon hide, she found her face pressed up against a fine, cool fabric and Galad's arms around her.

She looked up to see Galad clad in a long, pale blue tunic. He smiled. "Still curious?"

Of *course* she was—where had he summoned new clothing from, did he make them through magic, and had he just taken off his clothes for effect earlier? But what popped out of her mouth was, "Are you going to marry Mam?"

His face grew serious. "If that is what she wants." He touched her chin. "Is that what you want?"

A wave of longing rose in Aish that she had no words for. It made her throat burn, thinking about it, so she just shrugged and mumbled, "I wouldn't mind."

Galad's eyes grew very soft. "Let's go tell your Mam, then." With no effort at all, he swung her around to ride on his back. "Hold on," he said. He strode through the field and picked up his discarded clothing, seeming not to notice her weight at all.

Aish wrapped her arms around his neck and buried her face in his hair. She suspected all the things she had felt and couldn't say, he already knew.

CHAPTER

SEVEN

The next few weeks passed in a sweet tranquility the likes of which Roe could barely remember.

The corn grew, enriched with magic even though no rain fell. Aish did her chores with little complaint and smiled incessantly. And Galad… Galad made himself at home like he had always been there, in their house, and in her bed. Indeed, after so many years sleeping alone, often Roe had to shove him away in the night when he got too hot, because he did like to cuddle. Sometimes she didn't, though. Sometimes she just sweated in his arms and savored the novelty of being held.

After about three weeks, Roe was kneading the bread dough for the day when Fang, who had been dozing in front of the hearth, sat up and whined.

Roe hummed softly, folding the bread dough and covering the bowl with a cloth to rise.

Fang stood and whined again.

Dusting off her hands on her apron, Roe opened the door for him to go out. Fang shot out the doorway, but turned back, whining. "What is it?" Roe said, wiping a hand over her forehead.

Fang whined again, sharper and more insistent.

Roe stepped out into the yard and squinted up at the sky,

which was clear blue, not a cloud to be seen. "Why did I expect anything else," she mumbled, turning to go back in the house.

Fang barked and dashed forward to catch her skirt in his jaws.

"Fang, wha—"

A deep rumble came from the earth, growing in strength. Roe felt it in her bones, vibrating with enough strength to send her to the ground. The house trembled violently. She could see objects falling from shelves and dishes shattering on the floor through the open doorway. The goat and the chickens squawked in fear from the barn. Clutching the dog, she scooted into the center of the farmyard as the whole world shook.

Then, as suddenly as it had started, the rumble died away, leaving the earth still and her house full of broken crockery. Roe shakily got to her feet, hampered by Fang, who pressed himself to her leg, panting anxiously. She stared around in bewilderment. Everything looked exactly the same. Everything....

She blinked again and stared at the fields of corn, which had been so shiny and green that morning. Now she watched the green health and vitality in the stalks drain to withered brown before her eyes.

Her heart sank in her chest, even before Aish came running from the fields. "Mam! Mam!"

Roe's breath strangled in her throat.

Something's happened to Galad.

ROE FELL to her knees by Galad, Aish and Fang right behind her. He had fallen, Aish told her, when the earth had shaken, and he hadn't gotten up. He had been speaking a language she hadn't understood, so she went for help.

Roe could still hear Galad mumbling as he lay there, his eyes closed and his pallor gray. It sounded like the desert tongue. "Galad," she said loudly, so he would not be surprised, and pressed her hand to his forehead. "Galad," she said again.

He quieted under her touch, but still did not open his eyes.

"Aish, get some water—"

"No," he said hoarsely. "I am… well."

"You don't look well," she said bluntly.

He let out a weak laugh with little humor in it. His eyes were still closed.

"What happened? Do you know?"

"No, I do not know," he said bleakly. "I can only tell you what is happening now."

"And what's that?" she asked, but some part of her suspected the answer.

"The magic is gone," he said, and opened his eyes.

Roe heard Aish suck in her breath, but she kept still as Galad slowly levered himself to a sitting position. His eyes were blown wide and black, no white in them—a sign of deep distress, she realized, based on the last time he had appeared like this. She put a hand on his shoulder and helped.

"Someone has done… something," Galad said laboriously. "To the magic in the world." He stared bitterly at the withering cornstalks around them. They showed no sign of the care and tending he had given them over the past weeks. If anything, they looked worse. Then he turned and looked at Roe, and his expression changed to something like despair. "They have put it away, where I cannot reach it." He opened and closed his hands on nothing.

Roe sat back on her heels. "So… you won't be able to replenish the fields." Her heart sank. A lean harvest. Maybe they would be a little better off than their neighbors with three extra weeks of growing for their crops, able to salvage part of the corn crop at least. "Well, we'll all tighten our belts, I suppose. Get as many of the ears as we can and dry them, perhaps. Wasn't it a good thing I did some canning while the vegetable garden was still producing? We'll be all right. We…."

Galad was shaking his head.

"What?" she whispered.

"I cannot stay, Roe."

Her heart turned to lead in her chest.

"Dragons *need* magic. We depend on it, just like water or air to live. What little magic that remains here is draining away, going somewhere I cannot reach." He looked away from her, anguished. "I will not be able to stay with you."

"Where will you go?" Aish said, sounding lost.

"I must go south," he said, "to my people, to see if the deep wells of magic in the desert have drained dry. If they have not, then we will see how long they last. If they have, I will look for another place. Surely magic cannot be gone from everywhere in the world." He took her hand, keeping his eyes fixed on their entwined fingers. "I promised you that I would stay with you always," he said. "Know if there was any other way, I would not go back on my word. I do not *want* to go back on my word." His voice cracked.

Roe squeezed his hand. "How long can you safely stay?"

He said, in a voice of grief, "A few days, perhaps."

"Well, that's long enough. We'll sell the animals, and pack what's needed—should we pack for what we can carry, or what you can?"

He looked up at her, uncomprehending.

"Galad, you were willing to give up your home, your people, for us," Roe said gently, "for this little farm in the back end of Damaslar. I'm willing to do the same." She made a face at the corn. "We won't be able to live here, either."

"What are you saying?" he asked hoarsely.

"We will go with you, come what may." She took his face in her hands and kissed him. "If that's all right," she added hesitantly.

In answer, he pulled her to him, and his kiss nearly burned her to a cinder.

"Is that all right with you, little one?" he asked Aish once he had finished kissing the breath from Roe.

Her daughter looked from them to the farm where she had

spent her whole life. "Can we bring Fang?" she finally said in a tremulous voice.

Galad scratched the dog on the head. "Yes, we can bring Fang."

"Then I want to go." Aish brightened considerably. "Will we fly there? Can we ride you as a dragon?"

Galad dissolved into laughter. "She is asking questions again," he told Roe. "Everything will be all right."

IT DID NOT TAKE LONG to sell the nanny goat and the horse and chickens at bargain prices. Roe made a few halfhearted attempts to sell the land, but in this drought, no one was buying. The market was full of rumors of what caused the earth shakes—dire portents of things to come, along with the drought, most speculated—and other families were leaving the region as well, so their departure was not remarked on.

Galad used the coin he brought with him to buy leather to make a harness and carrying bags. He worked on it for two days while she and Aish packed their belongings, and on the third day, Roe watched him lay out the harness and transform into a dragon for the first time.

Fang pressed his belly to the ground and wagged his tail frantically as he whined. Roe pressed a hand to her mouth, staring in awe at the beautiful bronze wings that stretched open in the morning sunlight. They were at once strong and powerful but delicate. She could see the veins and tendons spanning the membranes between the wing's ribs.

"Come on, Fang, come see your basket," Aish said, taking the dog to get situated for travel.

Roe looked up into his whirling gold eyes and smiled. "You are a marvel."

"Thhhhhank you," he rumbled, which made her eyebrows shoot up, and then she laughed.

Roe and Aish tightened the harness straps to Galad's satisfaction, then loaded the baggage. With Fang settled in his basket, Aish scrambled up Galad's shoulder and settled safely into the padded leather that would be their seat, strapping in her legs. Roe sat behind her, surveying her farm from this added height. The fields where she had toiled for years, the house she had lived in with her husband, the place where she had given birth to her daughter. Her throat tightened.

Galad's head swiveled around to inspect them. "Sssssecure?" he said.

Roe pushed away the memories and tightened her leg straps. "Yes." She held tight to Aish as Galad pushed up from his crouch to his full height.

Memories traveled well. Everything she really needed was here with her, atop this dragon that had given her more than she'd ever hoped for.

"We're ready!" she called.

Roe laughed and whooped along with Aish as Galad took off at a run. With a powerful flap of his wings, he soared into the air, headed south to sand dunes and dragons and hopefully, magic. Headed home.

THANK you so much for reading! If you enjoyed this novella, please leave a review!!

Also by Claire Trella Hill

<u>Gothic Vampire Romance</u>

Black and Deep Desires

Parfit Gentil Knyght: an Addie and Etienne Vignette (Newsletter Exclusive)

<u>The Karneesia Chronicles</u>

The Erlking's Daughters

Mistress of Wardwood and Other Stories (Newsletter Exclusive)

The Flight of the Spellbound

<u>Tales from Karneesia</u>

When a Dragon Comes Courting

Come by Water

About the Author

Claire Trella Hill will read anything, but fantasy romance and gothic fiction are her favorites. Born and raised in Houston, Texas, she still lives there because she is impervious to 100 degree weather. She also has a bad habit of making her characters in the Sims and continuing their stories. When Claire isn't writing, she can be found with her nose glued to her library app, assisting with the last tricky pieces of a puzzle, swilling Dr. Pepper, collecting vintage romance covers, or cuddling with her cat.

You can connect with her on social media or sign up for her newsletter on her website ClaireTrellaHill.com.